The Baobab Tree

Retold by Louie Stowell

Illustrated by Laure Fournier

Reading Consultant: Alison Kelly
Roehampton University

This story is about a talking tree

and some angry
African gods.

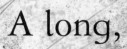

A long,

long,

long,

time ago

the gods made
the world.

5

One day, they made a talking tree.

They called it the Baobab* tree.

*say bay-oh-bab

The Baobab tree
talked a **lot**.

I don't like
this soil.

9

The gods grew a forest of tall trees.

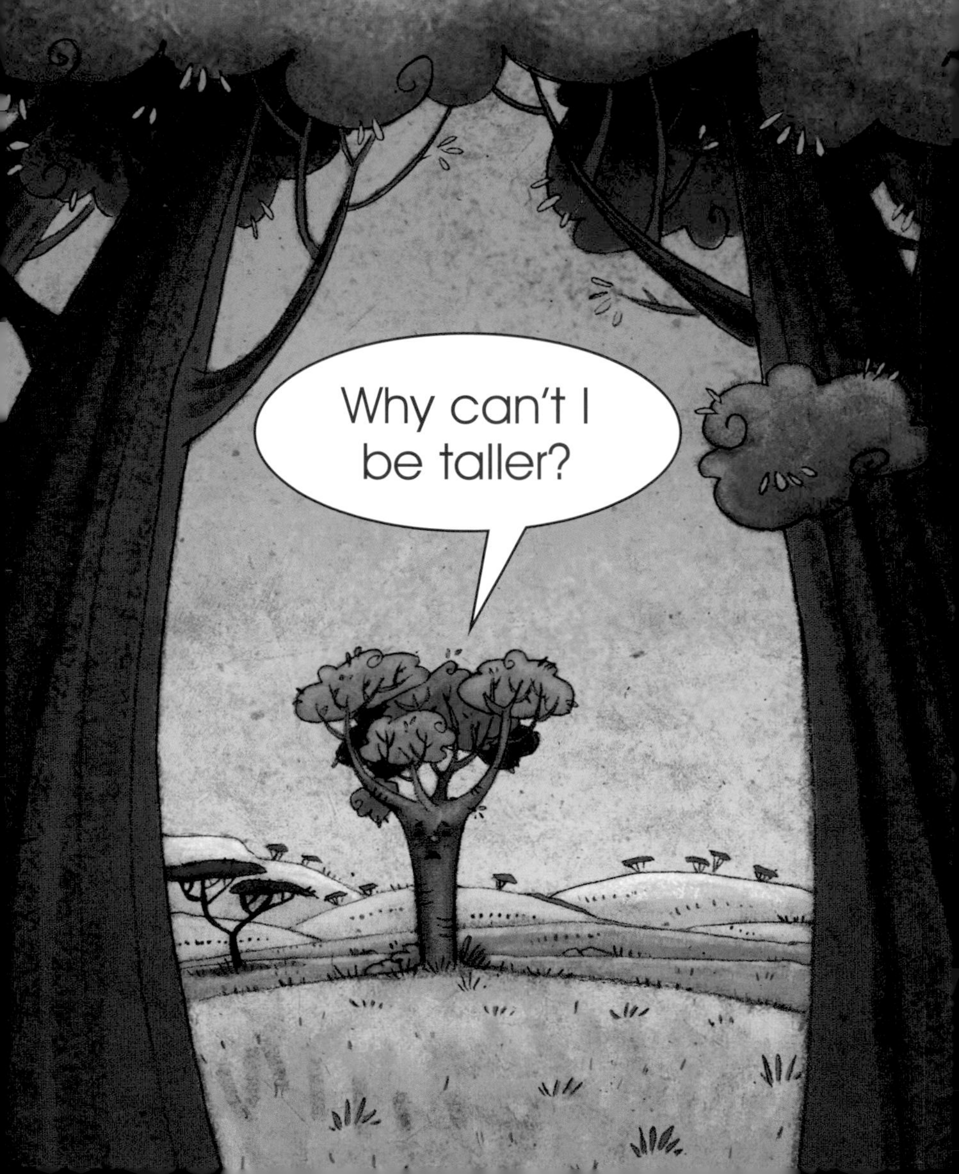

The Baobab tree
was fed up.

The gods made trees
with flowers.

The Baobab tree was
even more fed up.

Why don't I
have flowers?

The gods got cross.

"Stop moaning!" they said.

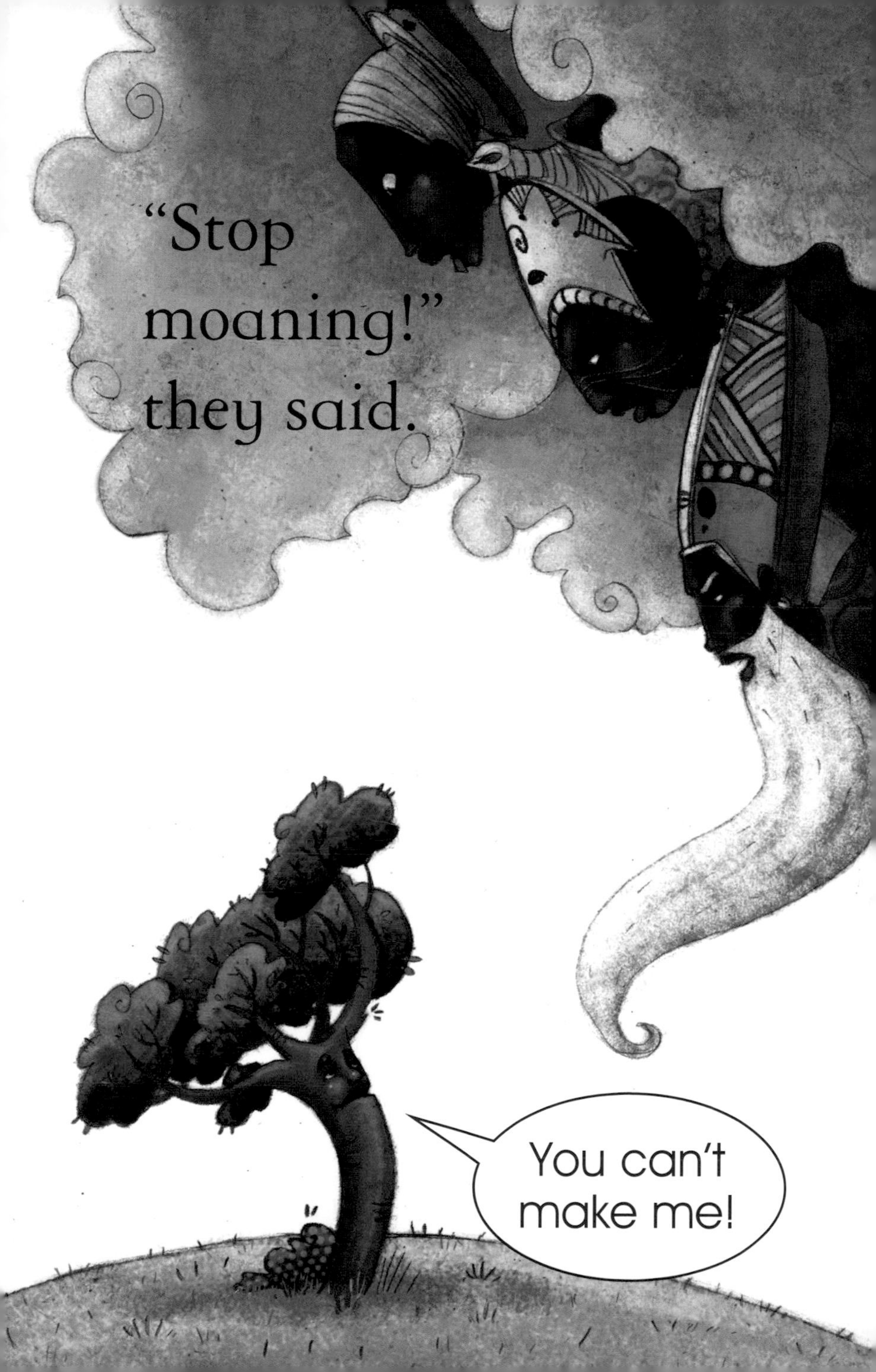

Then the gods made
trees that grew fruit.

"I want fruit," said the Baobab tree.

"Stop!"
cried the gods.

They grabbed the Baobab tree and turned it upside down.

Hey!

His head was in the
ground.

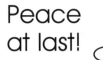

He couldn't open his
mouth to talk.

21

No one has ever heard
the Baobab tree say
another word.

PUZZLES

Puzzle 1

Put the pictures in order.

A   B   C

D   E   F

Puzzle 2
Spot the six differences
between these two pictures.

25

Puzzle 3
Can you spot five creatures hiding?

Puzzle 4

Match the sentences to the pictures.

"I'm thirsty."   "I'm cold."

"I want to be taller."   "It's too hot."

Answers to puzzles

Puzzle 1

E   A   F

B   D   C

Puzzle 2

Puzzle 3

bird

giraffe

rhino   elephant   zebra

Puzzle 4

"I want to be taller."

"It's too hot."

"I'm thirsty."

"I'm cold."

About
The Baobab Tree

This story is based on a
South African tale about a
tree known as the baobab.
The baobab tree looks as
if its roots are in the air, so
people came up with stories to
explain its strange shape.

Designed by Non Figg
Additional design by Emily Bornoff
Series designer: Russell Punter
Series editor: Lesley Sims

First published in 2009 by Usborne Publishing Ltd., Usborne House,
83-85 Saffron Hill, London EC1N 8RT, England. www.usborne.com
Copyright © 2009 Usborne Publishing Ltd.